BOOK ONE

A Story About Following God

In Search of
The Great
White Tiger

by SHEILA WALSH

illustrations by DON SULLIVAN

A CHILDREN OF FAITH BOOK *published by* WATERBROOK PRESS

This book is for every child,
young or old,
whose heart longs to know
the unconditional love of God.

IN SEARCH OF THE GREAT WHITE TIGER
PUBLISHED BY WATERBROOK PRESS
2375 Telstar Drive, Suite 160
Colorado Springs, Colorado 80920
A division of Random House, Inc.

ISBN 1-57856-333-X

Copyright © 2001 by Sheila Walsh

Illustrations copyright © 2001 by Don Sullivan

Gnoo Zoo characters copyright © 2001 by Aslan Entertainment and Children of Faith

Published in association with the literary agency of Alive Communications, Inc.,
7680 Goddard Street, Suite 200, Colorado Springs, CO 80920.

The executive producer of Gnoo Zoo is Stephen Arterburn, M.Ed.
Children of Faith, 436 Main Street, Suite 205, Franklin, TN 37064

Visit Children of Faith at http://children-of-faith.com

Library of Congress Cataloging-in-Publication Data
Walsh, Sheila, 1956-
    In search of the Great White Tiger / by Sheila Walsh; illustrations by Don Sullivan.—
1st ed.
        p. cm.—(Gnoo Zoo)
    Summary: When the carousel animals are taken prisoner by the evil Reptillion, they turn
for help to the Great White Tiger, who made the Land of Gnoo.
        ISBN 1-57856-333-X
    [1. Fantasy.] I. Sullivan, Don, 1953- ill. II. Title. III. Series.

PZ7.W16894 In 2001
[Fic]—dc21
                                                            00-068523

Printed in the United States of America
2001—First Edition

10 9 8 7 6 5 4 3 2 1

A Note to Parents

"Mommy, what is God like?"

I looked into the large brown eyes of my three-year-old son, Christian, and thought for a few moments.

"He is wonderful, darling. He is all that is good. He made you and he always loves you."

Christian sat with that thought.

"Even when I'm naughty?"

"Yes."

"Even if I'm very naughty?"

"Yes."

"Cool!"

He ran off to chase the cat around the dining-room table, and I wondered if I had just presented my son with a lifelong get-out-of-jail-free card. But that's the tension of the gospel, the wonder, the outrageous greatness of the love of God: Whether we are naughty or nice, he loves us unconditionally.

In 1998 a short conversation with a woman became a turning point in my life. I imagine she was in her seventies. She had attended a Women of Faith conference and heard me speak on God's radical love. At the end of the evening, she stood before me with tears pouring down her cheeks.

"I have gone to church all my life," she said, "but tonight is the first time I have truly understood that God loves me."

I thought about that for a long time. How would her life have been affected if she had understood God's love *as a child?*

And so the vision for Children of Faith was born. It is our heart, our passion, to build into the foundation stones of our sons' and daughters' lives the wonder of the love of God, the beauty of truth and grace.

In this first book we introduce the Land of Gnoo, our earth packaged in allegorical wonder, a *Pilgrim's Progress* for little ones. Our pilgrims here know that they have been made in the image of God, the Great White Tiger, because every one of them has been sealed with his pawprint. They embark on a journey to find him, and along the way they encounter Reptillion, the enemy who will do anything to stop them. Our friends make many mistakes and wrong choices, but they discover that the one who loves them has been watching over them all along. They are changed by the lessons they learn.

I can think of no greater privilege than the joy of communicating God's heart toward children. I believe that when we finally understand we are loved enough to be given that lifelong get-out-of-jail-free ticket, our lives will be forever changed. Rather than claiming license to live as we please, we will discover our calling to live in such a way that pleases and honors the one who loves us so much.

Thank you for inviting us into your hearts and homes. It is a sacred trust. And so we begin our journey…

Do you ever wonder if God sees you?
Is he watching when you play
and when your day is through?
Come now with our travelers—
for they ask that question too—
and you'll hear the Great White Tiger's roar:

"Yes, I love you!"

CHAPTER ONE

On a brand-new morning in a faraway land called Gnoo, which only a few have ever visited, someone was watching as dozens of children poured through the Grand Gnoo Gates and came running to the amazing carousel called the Gnoo Zoo.

"Mommy, look at this skinny old bird!" cried a boy as he climbed onto the ostrich's back.

"Oooh! I want this one!" said a girl, hugging the panda's neck with sticky, cotton-candy fingers.

When every child was ready at last, a large golden key slowly turned at the center of the Gnoo Zoo, and the music and the motion began.

All day long the children rode the animals round and round—as round and round the world goes. All day long, they sang to the Gnoo Zoo music:

"We love Gnoo, where dreams come true.

We love Gnoo; we're happy, too!

We love Gnoo; nowhere else will do,

for the White Tiger made the Land of Gnoo."

And all day long, that someone—whose name was Big Billy— kept watching the children's happy faces...

...until the day was over, and every sleepy girl and boy finally left the Gnoo Zoo and disappeared, one by one, through the slowly closing Grand Gnoo Gates.

And then,
    when the gates closed with a "click!"
        and everything fell silent and still...

...the animals came to life! The shiny pole twisted up from Big Billy's back, and he stood and stretched and smiled. "What a day!" he said. "What a scrumptiously wonderful day!"

"Well, speak for yourself," said the ostrich. "I've never been so insulted in all my life. 'Skinny old bird' indeed! Humph! I'm streamlined, not skinny."

"Come on, Miss Marbles," Big Billy said. "Think of it as a compliment. After all, the boy did choose *you* to ride on, didn't he?"

Miss Marbles flashed her long eyelashes. "Well, of course I am irrrrresistible. How totally true!"

"How totally silly," said Chattaboonga the monkey, stretching out to high-five her twin sister, Boongachatta. "If only everyone were as cool as we are!" she said.

"We're cool! We're cool!" the sisters crowed together.

"Did someone say she's cool?" asked Einstein the elephant. "Seems quite warm to me tonight."

"Oh brother!" said Chattaboonga. "You'd think you could hear, with those great flapping ears!"

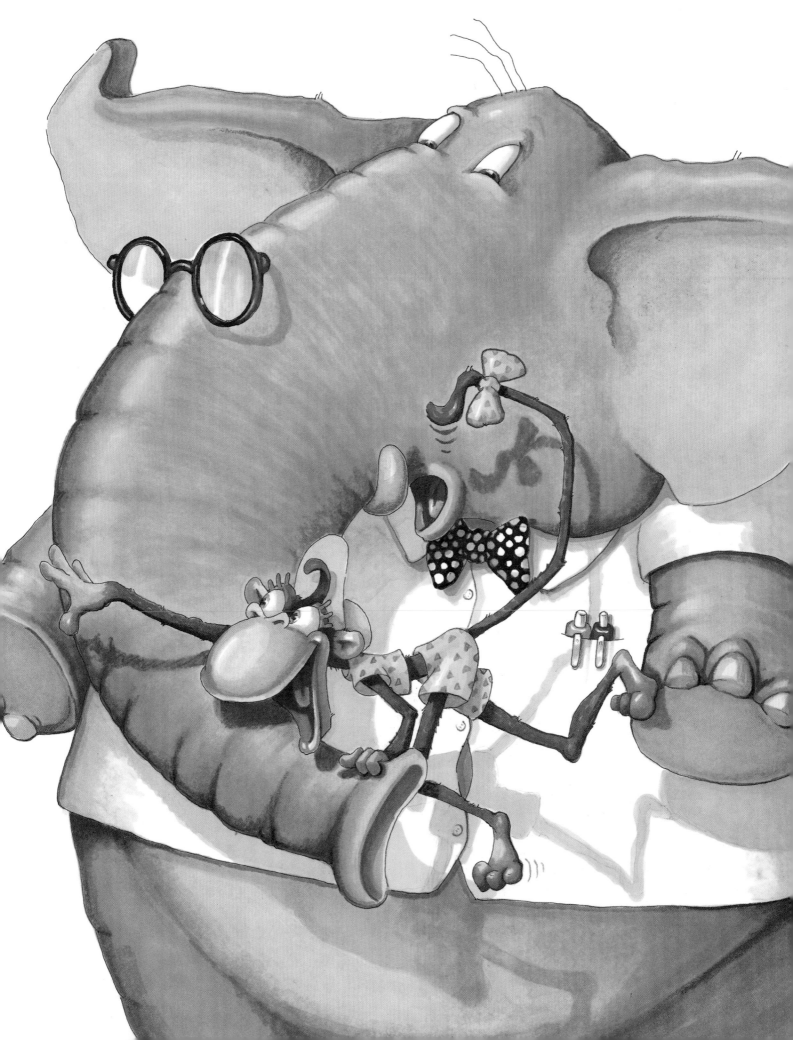

Heh heh! Just you wait!

Einstein laughed with everyone as they danced and sang under the golden Gnoo moon:

"We love Gnoo, where dreams come true.

We love Gnoo; we're happy, too!

We love Gnoo; nowhere else will do,

for the White Tiger made the Land of Gnoo."

Big Billy could think of nothing he'd rather do than enjoy his friends forever at the Gnoo Zoo.

But suddenly a huge shadow blocked the moonlight, and a terrible roar filled the sky. The ground shook, and the carousel creaked and groaned.

Out of the darkness, a horrible monster stormed up to the animals. "I am Reptillion! I am the new master of the carousel," he snarled. "Now you all belong to me!"

"Oh, but that could *never* be true!" Big Billy said. Although his knees trembled, he stepped forward bravely. "We belong to the Great White Tiger. See! Look at our paws."

"Aahhrrghh!" Reptillion roared in anger, and quicker than a butterfly's blink he grabbed Boongachatta's outstretched paw and took her prisoner for his lunchbox.

"Aaahhhrrrghhh!" Reptillion roared again, and all the spindly poles descended, holding the animals fast once more.

Reptillion crawled onto the carousel, snatched the golden key, and swallowed it. "No more music!" he screamed. "And no more laughter! I hate happy people!"

He turned to the horrible creature at his side. "Creepshaw," he snarled, "guard these miserable animals while I'm away. There will be no singing! No smiling! And most of all, never let them mention that huge, white...*aahhrrghh!*"

Reptillion stomped out into the darkness, carrying a kicking and screaming Boongachatta. "Help! Big Billy, help me!"

"I'll never see my sister again!" Chattaboonga cried.

Miss Marbles took her best lace handkerchief from her purse and gave it to the monkey.

"Quiet!" Creepshaw shouted.

So Miss Marbles whispered, "Big Billy, what do we do now?"

"Yes, Big Billy," whispered Einstein, "what now?"

"Yes, Big Billy," sniffled Chattaboonga, "what now?"

"Silence!" yelled Creepshaw, picking at his teeth with a toothpick.

The animals stayed quiet the rest of the night, but Big Billy didn't sleep a wink. Not one wink.

When morning arrived, the children came running to the carousel, only to turn and walk sadly away.

"Mommy, it's broken!" a small boy cried. "There's no key! No music! No Gnoo Zoo!"

Later that day, when Creepshaw finally took an afternoon nap, the animals whispered again, "What are we going to do, Big Billy? What are we going to do?"

"I think..." Big Billy said slowly, while Creepshaw snored, "I think there is only one who can help us now. It is the *Great...White...Tiger.*"

"Don't say that name!" screamed Creepshaw, almost swallowing his toothpick. "Never say that name! Never, NEVER, *NEVER!*"

He raced round and round the carousel, lashing the animals with his long sticky tongue until he got quite dizzy and had to hold on to Big Billy's pole. The animals trembled.

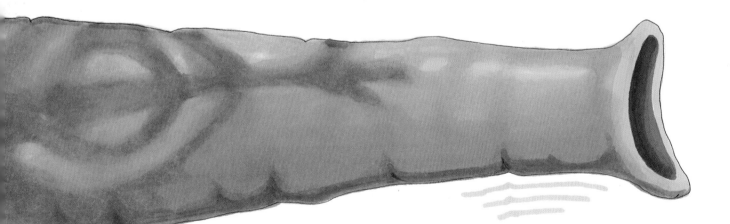

It was a long time before Creepshaw
finally settled back into his nap.

Now all the animals were afraid even to whisper. Big Billy looked into the sky, and in the smallest voice a big panda bear can make, he said, "Great White Tiger, one who loves us, help us now, for we need you."

And so another day came to an end, but that evening there was no singing and no laughter at the Gnoo Zoo. The animals cried themselves to sleep.

They were awakened by a deep, loud *bark, bark, bark!*

Someone was flying above the carousel.

"The name's Lou," he said. "Got a message for you from the G. W. T. himself. He says to come see him—though I gotta warn you: The trip's gonna be tough. Reeeeeaal tough. So speak up. Who wants to give it a shot?"

"We do!" cried Big Billy and Miss Marbles and Chattaboonga and Einstein with excitement.

"Do you think the Great White Tiger has any chocolate?" Einstein whispered to Big Billy. Chocolate was Einstein's favorite food. "I haven't had any for soooo long."

They had so many questions for Lou, but before they could ask even one, he reached out and made their poles disappear.

Creepshaw began groaning in his sleep.

"Let's hit it, everybody!" Lou commanded. "Let's get out of here before that sleeping creep wakes up."

"But which way do we go?" Big Billy asked.

"Whoa," answered Lou. "Good point. Almost forgot. Here's what the G. W. T. himself says:

> *'If free and happy you would be,*
>
> *take the path that leads to me—*
>
> *not the easy way ahead;*
>
> *choose the harder road instead.'*

So take 'em there, Billy Bear! You can do it!"

And with that, Lou went skiddoo!

Creepshaw was now spluttering and muttering and smacking his skinny lips.

Big Billy scurried at once into the Do-Gnoo Woods. "Follow me!" he shouted. And that's just what his friends did.

They're gone, you fool!

CHAPTER THREE

They didn't stop running until they came to a wide, rushing river. The path stopped there and continued on the other side. A rope stretched out before them; they could cross the river by hanging on to it. But they also saw something else.

"Oh, look!" said Miss Marbles. "A ship!"

"Well actually, Miss Marbles," Einstein said, "technically, it's a canoe. A blue canoe." He liked to be accurate.

"Everyone climb aboard," Miss Marbles ordered. "I'll drive. I love to cruise! This will be *easy!*"

"Easy?" said Big Billy. "But remember our message from the Great White Tiger?

    'Choose the harder road instead.'

Maybe we should just use the rope."

"Nonsense," said Miss Marbles. "My necklace could get tangled in the rope, and I simply can't get my purse wet. Hurry aboard, everyone!" she said. "That nasty Creepshaw might come after us."

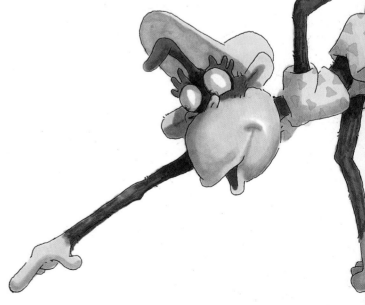

So everyone climbed in. But soon the choppy river water filled the overloaded canoe.

"We're sinking!" cried Chattaboonga.

"My lovely purse is soaked!" cried Miss Marbles.

"Big Billy, we've hit quite a snafu!" cried Einstein.

"Help us, Great White Tiger!" cried Big Billy. *"Help us!"*

Just as the water reached their necks, they heard a calm voice above them saying, "Hold on, everyone. Hold on!"

A flying horse carried them back to shore, where she told them her name was Lulu.

"Please tell me, Big Billy," Lulu asked, "why didn't you use the rope to get across?"

Big Billy shivered and sneezed. He couldn't stop his teeth from chattering. "I'm s-s-so s-s-sorry," he answered. "The boat s-s-seemed s-s-safe."

"Ah, but the safest thing," said Lulu, "is to always do what the Great White Tiger asks." As Lulu flew off into the sky, she called back, "He loves you more than enough to keep you safe!"

When Big Billy had finally stopped shivering, he led his friends across the rope as fast as they could go.

A little water won't stop us, eh Boss?

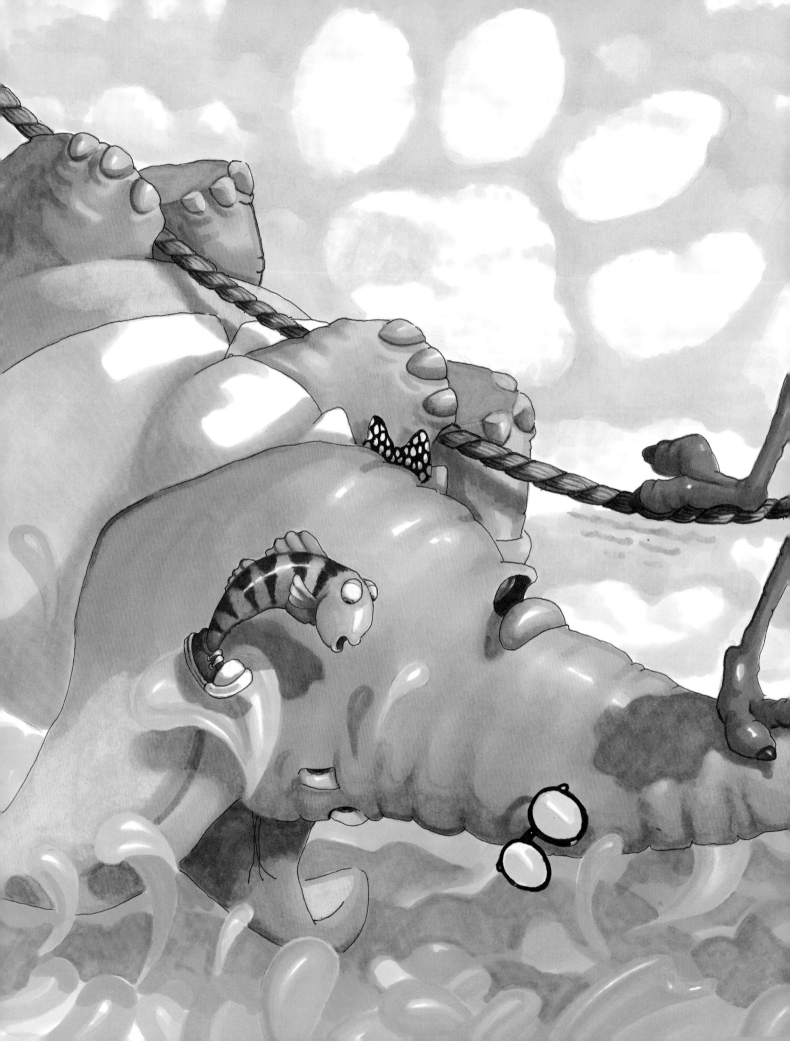

CHAPTER FOUR

On the other side of the river, they followed the path through the Do-Gnoo Woods. They were all dry now and so happy that they danced and sang.

"We believe in the Great White Tiger.

We believe that his words are true.

We will follow his path forever,

singing and dancing—how we love you!"

They stopped singing when their path split in two, each leading to a tunnel in Rendezvoo Mountain.

"How do we decide which tunnel to take?" Miss Marbles asked Big Billy.

"Oh," said Einstein before Big Billy could answer, "that's quite easy. Look! We'll follow these footprints. Anyway, this tunnel on the left does look brighter. I've always been afraid of the dark. Unless it's dark chocolate," he added. "That's my favorite."

"Afraid? A big boy like you?" said Chattaboonga. "But remember the Great White Tiger's words?

   'Choose the harder road instead.'"

Miss Marbles added, "Besides, my glorious necklace has glow-in-the-dark pearls. The darker it is, the more beautiful they'll be."

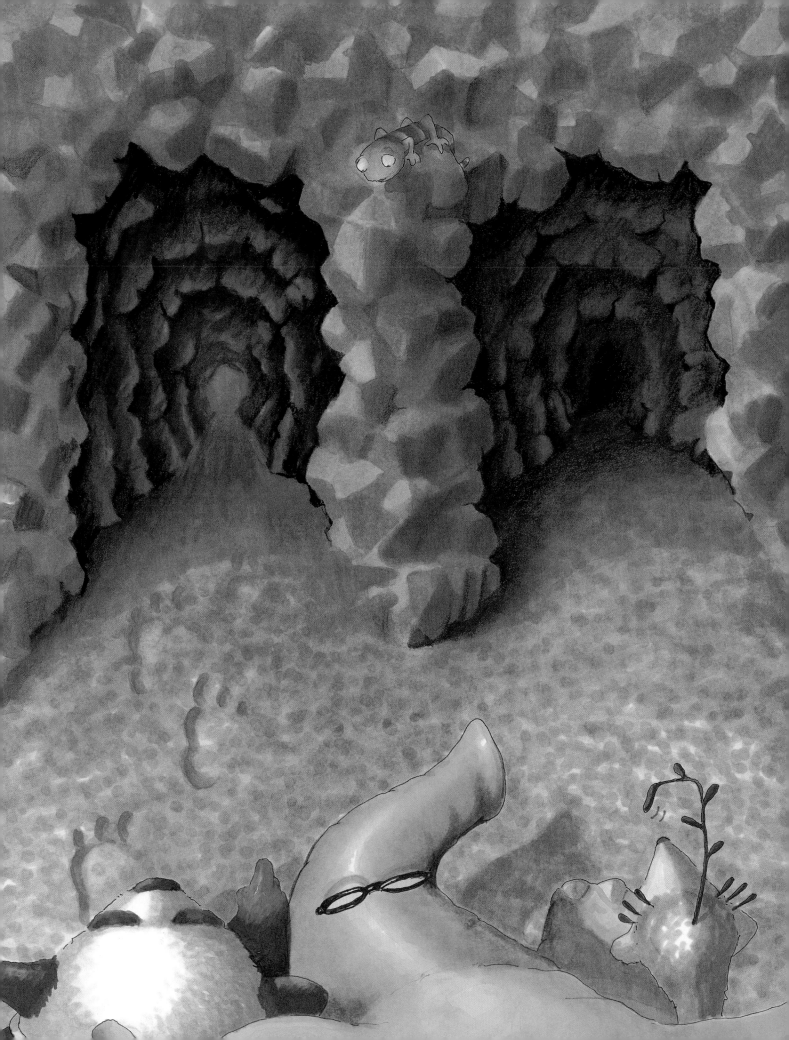

But Einstein had already followed the footprints into the cave on the left. Big Billy and the others came right behind him.

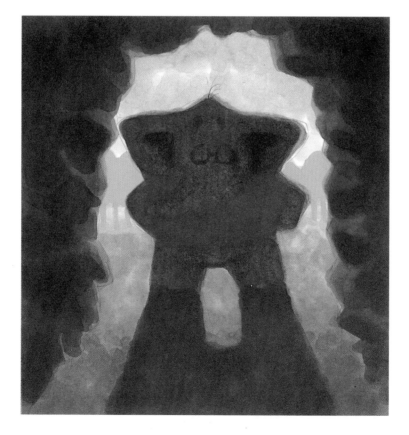

Suddenly an iron gate came crashing down. Out of the shadows jumped Reptillion and Creepshaw.

"You're trapped!" Reptillion shouted. "This is no tunnel! It's a cave—and it's your grave! Creepshaw and I will take our torches and leave you here forever!"

"What?" cried Einstein. "In the *d-d-d-dark?*"

"Yes!" laughed Reptillion. "Yes! In the dark *forever!*"

"No! No!" shouted Big Billy as bravely as he could. "This is all my fault," he said with tears running down his fur. "I should have led my friends the other way. Reptillion, I will be your prisoner forever. I deserve nothing more, but please let my friends go. I beg you!"

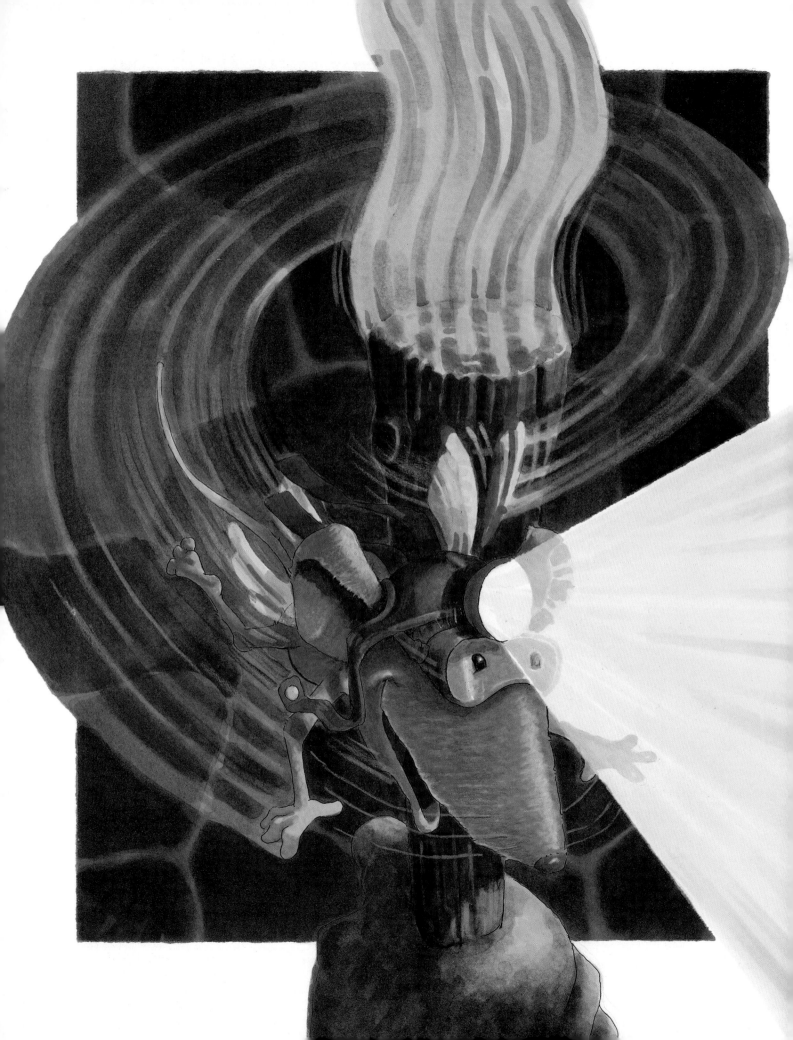

All at once they heard a strange buzzing sound, and a squeaky voice called out, "Splendid, Big Billy! I say, just splendid!" A flying mouse wearing a headlamp was buzzing around Reptillion and Creepshaw. He snuffed out their torches, then flew in their faces and turned his lamp on high beam. "Dipsey-do!" he squeaked. It blinded the eyes of Reptillion and Creepshaw, and they stumbled and crashed into the cave walls.

"Toodaloo here," the mouse said to Big Billy and his friends. Toodaloo's small teeth were like a buzz saw, and he quickly cut a hole through the iron gate. "This way, everybody!" he told them. "Tally ho!"

"I was waiting for you in the tunnel next door," Toodaloo explained, as he led them out of the cave and into the right tunnel. His headlamp lit their path inside. "Just as I was changing batteries in this old bonnet of mine, I heard such a ruckus coming from the cave next door! Well, I shot over just in time to hear Big Billy talking. Good show, young man! Quite willing to give your life for your friends! You've made the Great White Tiger jolly glad! What a fine chap you are!"

For hours, Toodaloo kept on cheerfully talking until they finally came out the tunnel's end on the other side of Rendezvoo Mountain.

There before them was a maze with hundreds of twists and turns. Another path led around to the right, smooth and straight, with no obstacles. Which way should they go?

They remembered the Great White Tiger's words and said them aloud all together:

"*Choose the harder road instead.*"

Stepping inside the maze, Big Billy sighed. "This road looks too hard!" he complained.

"And my feet are killing me," moaned Miss Marbles.

"Oh come on, chaps, do cheer *up!*" said Toodaloo. "Cheer up...and look up!" A huge bird circled right above them.

"That's Bartholomew," Toodaloo said. "Now listen carefully to the Great White Tiger's instructions:

'*When Bartholomew moves, you move.*

When Bartholomew stops, you stop.'

Ta-ta," Toodaloo called, and he flew away before they could ask him any questions.

CHAPTER FIVE

Above them, Bartholomew quickly flew onward. Big Billy and the others had to hurry through the maze to keep up. Wherever Bartholomew turned, they turned—and turned and turned and turned...

Follow them footsteps!

This had been a very long day, and now night was taking over as gray clouds filled the sky.

Einstein was worried. "It's getting so dark!" he cried. "I can hardly see Bartholomew!"

"Me either!" cried Chattaboonga.

"How simply dreadful!" cried Miss Marbles.

But Big Billy was calm. "The Great White Tiger loves us," he said. "Somehow he'll show us the way."

"Look!" Big Billy cried. "Just look! Bartholomew's wings are glowing!"

But only Big Billy could see them; the others were too frightened to look up and see.

"What about us?" Einstein cried.

"I know!" Miss Marbles said. She took off her glow-in-the-dark pearl necklace so everyone could hold on to it. Big Billy stayed in front following Bartholomew.

"Move faster!" Chattaboonga whispered. "I think I hear someone behind us!"

At that moment, Bartholomew suddenly stopped flying
forward and turned in a tight circle straight above them.
Big Billy stopped so suddenly that Miss Marbles crashed
into him, and Einstein crashed into Miss Marbles.

"No!" shouted Chattaboonga. "Don't stop now!
I hear them! They're right behind us! They'll
catch me like they did my sister! Go! GO! GO!" she screamed.

Big Billy was shaking in fear. "I *can't* go," he said. "This
time we *must* obey the Great White Tiger's instructions!"

Suddenly a fierce wind blew the clouds away. The beautiful glowing Gnoo moon covered everything with light. Now that he could see, Big Billy gasped. He had stopped right on the edge of a cliff. If he had taken one more step, he would have plunged over the edge and taken all his friends with him.

They all drew back, and Big Billy fell to his knees. His eyes filled with tears. "Thank you, Great White Tiger!" he said.

Above him a voice like thunder answered, "You are welcome, little one!"

Big Billy looked up. There before him was the Great White Tiger! "Oh, we found you!" Big Billy exclaimed.

The Tiger's deep voice answered, "I've been with you all the time."

Then the Great White Tiger roared into the sky: "Bring me the enemies!"

From high above, Bartholomew flew down clutching Reptillion and Creepshaw. He dropped them before the Great White Tiger.

"Give Boongachatta to me," the Tiger ordered. *"Now!"*

Reptillion dropped his lunchbox to the ground, and out jumped Boongachatta.

"Whew! That could cramp a girl's style," she said with a grin.

To Reptillion and Creepshaw, the Great White Tiger commanded, "Be gone!"

At the sound of his great voice they stumbled backward, then fell over the cliff.

"I'll be baaaack!" Reptillion screamed as he fell.

Then the Tiger turned to Big Billy. "What have you learned on your journey, my son?"

"I've learned to love my friends," Big Billy answered. "And I've learned to love and trust you, Great Tiger."

The Tiger's roar filled the air. "My son," he said, "you have learned a great deal. You will have much to give and to share when you return to the Gnoo Zoo to bring back the music and the laughter."

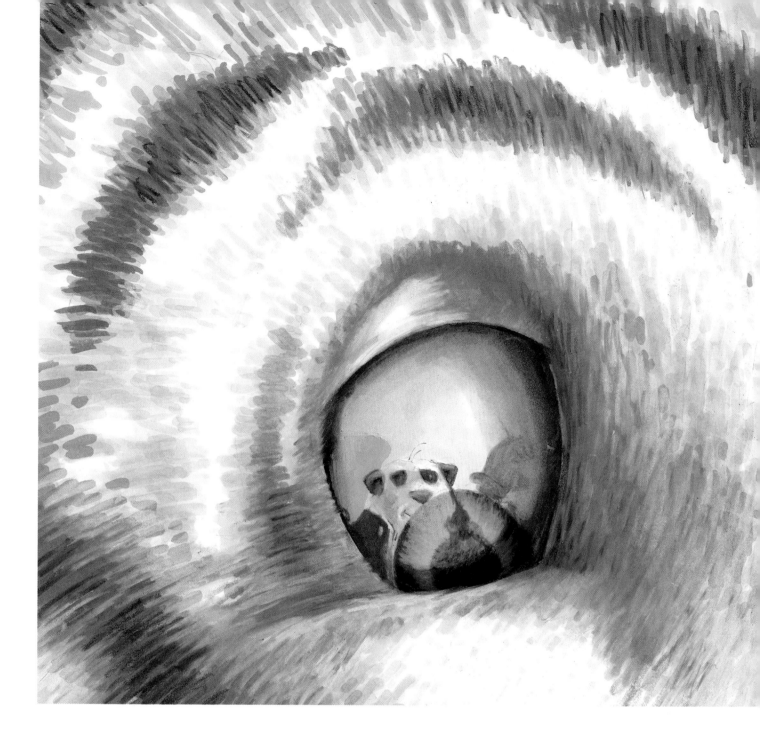

"But," Big Billy said, "if I may ask you, Great Tiger, how can we bring back the music? Reptillion swallowed the golden key."

"There is a better key," the Tiger answered. "The True Gnoo Key. You will find it when you continue your journey—if you

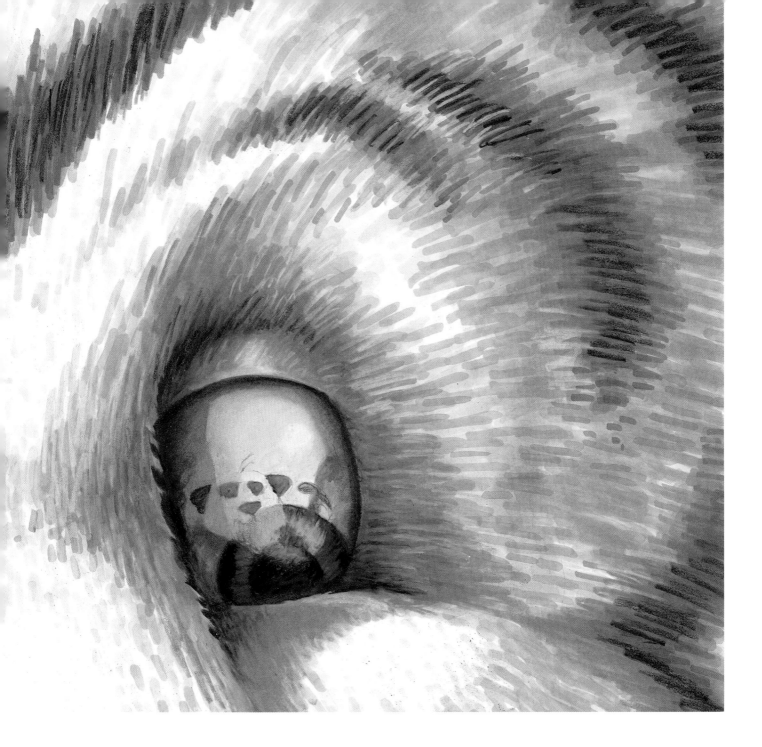

choose to go. Then you can return and help those left behind on the carousel.

"I must warn you, little ones: The journey from here will be more difficult than ever. But I will always be with you. So tell me: Who will go?"

"We will!" cried Big Billy and Miss Marbles and Einstein and Chattaboonga and Boongachatta.

"Could I have some chocolate for the trip?" Einstein asked timidly.

"And can we party before we go?" asked Boongachatta. "I've been lunch meat so long, I'm ready to *dance!*"

"Of course!" the Great White Tiger roared with joy.

All at once the sky was filled with the songs of the Great White Tiger and with his messengers, who sang:

"How we love you, Great White Tiger!

How we love the things you do!

You are good and kind and fearless.

You love us, and we love you!"